10/02

Jenny's Bear

by Michael Ratnett
illustrated by June Goulding

G. P. Putnam's Sons   New York

For Caroline,
and the bears

Text copyright © 1991 by Michael Ratnett
Illustrations © 1991 by June Goulding
First American Edition published in 1992 by
G. P. Putnam's Sons, a division of The Putnam & Grosset Book Group,
200 Madison Avenue, New York, NY 10016.
Originally published in Great Britain in 1991 by Hutchinson
Children's Books, London. Published simultaneously in Canada.
Printed in Belgium. Book design by ACE Limited.

Library of Congress Cataloging-in-Publication Data
Ratnett, Michael. Jenny's bear/Michael Ratnett :
illustrated by June Goulding.—1st American ed.   p.   cm.
Summary: Jenny loves all of the hundreds of toy bears
that she owns, but what she wants most in the world is
to meet a real, live bear.
[1. Bears—Fiction. 2. Toys—Fiction.]
I. Goulding, June, ill.   II. Title.
PZ7.R1938Je   1992   [E]—dc20   91-24051 CIP AC
ISBN 0-399-22325-8
1 3 5 7 9 10 8 6 4 2
First American Edition

Jenny had hundreds of bears of all shapes and sizes,
and she loved them all. But what she wanted most
in all the world was to meet a real live bear.

"Mom," she said one morning, "if we made a nice, cozy sort of den in the shed, would a real bear come and live in it?"

"I don't think so," Mom said kindly. "There aren't any real bears around here."

"Not even if I wished very hard?" asked Jenny.

"I'm afraid not," said Mom. "But we can make a den just for you and your toy bears, if you like."

The shed was in a terrible state.

"Phew," said Mom, "I've never seen such a mess. It must be years since this place was last cleaned!"

"It's no wonder that there aren't any bears living around here if all the sheds are this messy," said Jenny seriously.

"No wonder at all," said Mom.

When the den was ready, Jenny moved her bears in
so that if a real bear did come, he would feel right at home.
   "There," she said. "You look just right. Now, I've got
to go in for lunch, so you'll have to keep watch for me,
and if a bear does turn up, be sure to make him feel welcome."

All through lunch Jenny kept wishing for a real bear to be waiting for her back in the den.

And then she hurried out to the shed with a tray full of special things for the bear to eat.

But the den was just as she had left it. There was no sign of a real bear anywhere.

"Phooey!" said Jenny.

But she set out her tea things and her books just the same, and then sat down to wait patiently.

Jenny and her bears waited, and waited and waited. And just when it seemed that nobody was ever coming, there was a knock at the door.

"Come in," said Jenny.

And in stepped the biggest, brownest, friendliest-looking bear she had ever seen!

"Hello," he said. "I hope you don't mind me popping in, but I've come all the way from the Wild North, searching for somewhere to spend the winter, and this is by far the coziest-looking place I've found."

"Of course I don't mind," said Jenny. "I made this den specially for bears, and I've been wishing for a bear all day."

Then Jenny sat the bear down, and told him to help himself to the food. He had cakes, cookies and custard, which he thought was wonderfully wobbly. But he was not at all sure about the tea Jenny poured out for him.

"Hmm," he said. "This cup doesn't look very full. What kind of tea is it?"

"It's *pretend* tea," said Jenny.

"Oh, that's all right then," said the bear. " Pretend tea is the kind that bears like best."

And he drank it all up in one sip. "Another cup, please," he said, "but not so much sugar this time, thank you."

Then Jenny showed the bear her books.

"Which one would you like first?" she asked. "The happy one or the sad one?"

"The sad one," said the bear. " As long as it's not too sad."

But it was too sad.

"Boohoo, boohoo," blubbered the bear. "Stop it. You're making me cry!" And big tears ran down his furry face.

So Jenny read the funny story to cheer him up.

"Ho ho ho!" roared the bear. "No more, no more. My sides are going to split!" And they both rolled around on the floor until the whole shed shook.

"That was fun," said the bear. "What shall we do now?"

"I've got this," said Jenny, holding up a small bottle.

"Bubbles!" said the bear. "However did you guess? All bears love blowing bubbles."

Outside Jenny and the bear blew hundreds of shimmering bubbles.

"You're very good at this," said Jenny.

"My whole family are champion bubble-blowers," said the bear. "My grandad once blew a bubble that was so big it took him right up into the air and carried him hundreds of miles away."

"Wow!" said Jenny. "Did he ever get home again?"

"Oh yes, " said the bear. "He wrapped himself in brown paper and mailed himself back. He was a very clever bear."

By the end of the day, Jenny and the bear were the closest of friends. So Jenny was very sad when the bear said that it was time for him to go.

"But you said you were going to stay for the winter," she said.

"Yes," said the bear. "It's not winter yet though, and I've got lots of things to do first."

"You will come back, won't you?" said Jenny. "And bring your friends."

"I'll try," said the bear. "But remember to keep wishing."

Then he gave Jenny a special bear hug, and set off
down the road. Jenny waved until the bear was out of sight,
and went indoors for supper.

The next morning Jenny jumped out of bed, dressed quickly, and ran out to the shed.

But the den was empty. The big brown bear
who liked stories and blowing bubbles was not there.
  "What's the matter?" asked Mom.
  "My bear's gone," said Jenny.
  "Cheer up," said Mom, "you know there wasn't
really a bear, don't you?"

The weeks went by, and the weather got colder; but though there was still no sign of the bear, Jenny didn't forget him.

"There *was* a bear," she said to herself. "And he will come back. I just have to keep wishing."

Then one morning, Jenny drew back the curtains, looked
out the window, and saw something magical in the
snowy garden. She tugged on her coat and boots, and
ran out for a better look.

"A Snowbear!" she gasped.

And then she saw the huge prints in the snow. She followed them all the way to the shed.

Everything was quite silent as she carefully pushed open the door...

"SURPRISE!" roared a chorus of growly voices. The shed was crowded with bears – real bears of every shape and size. And right in the middle sat Jenny's bear!

"I said I'd come back," he said. "And this time I've brought the tea, and there's plenty for everyone."

'What kind of tea?' laughed Jenny.
  'Why pretend, of course,' said the bear.
  'Oh, good,' said Jenny. "That's the kind I like best!"